For Amy and Landry

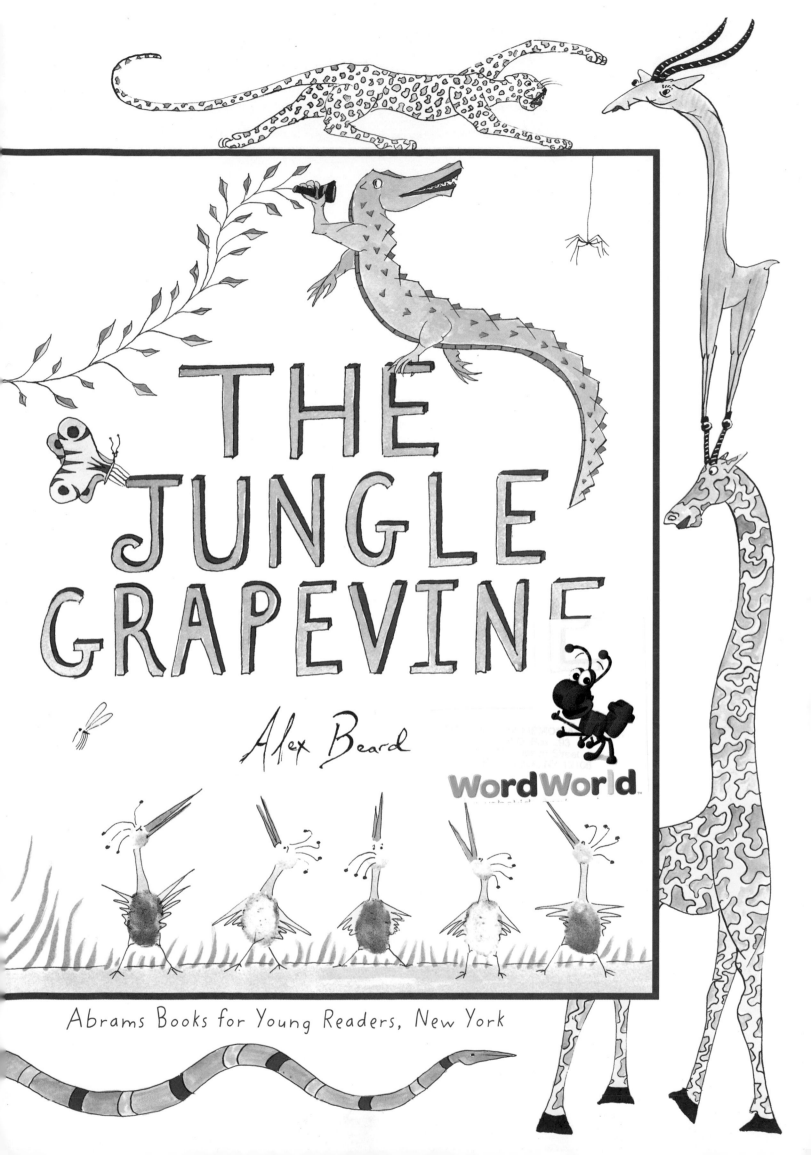

THE JUNGLE GRAPEVINE

Alex Beard

WordWorld

Abrams Books for Young Readers, New York

Turtle and Bird walked under the African sun.

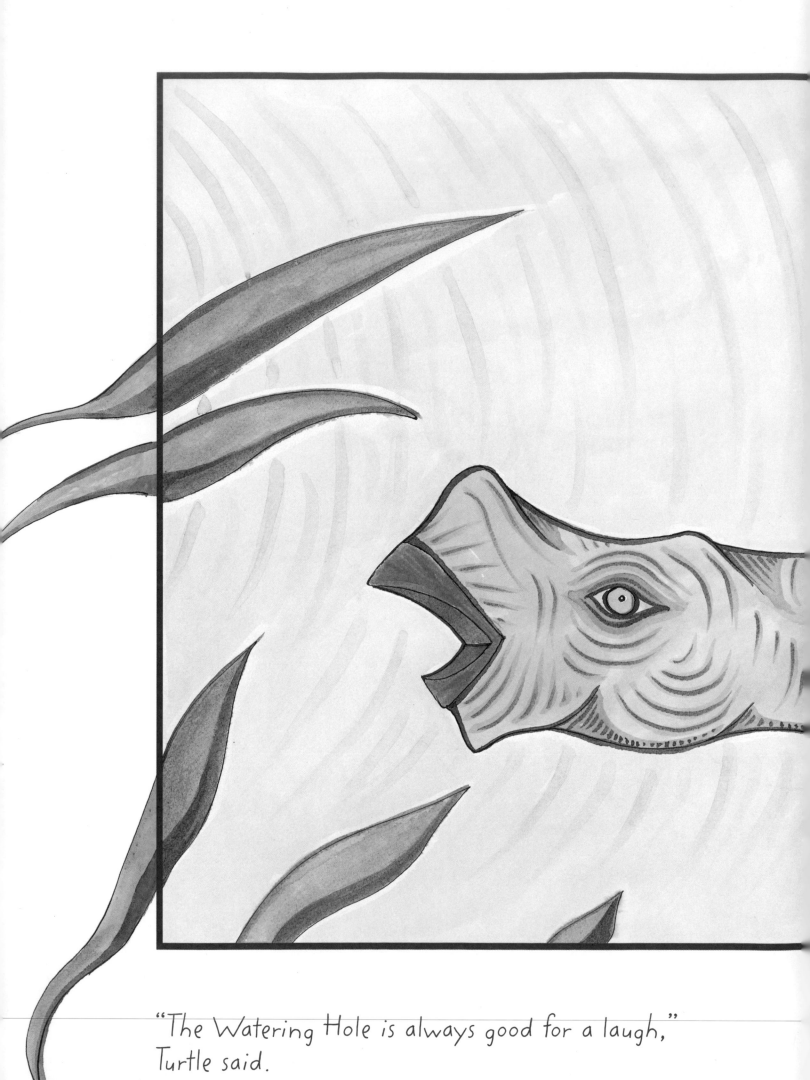

"The Watering Hole is always good for a laugh,"
Turtle said.

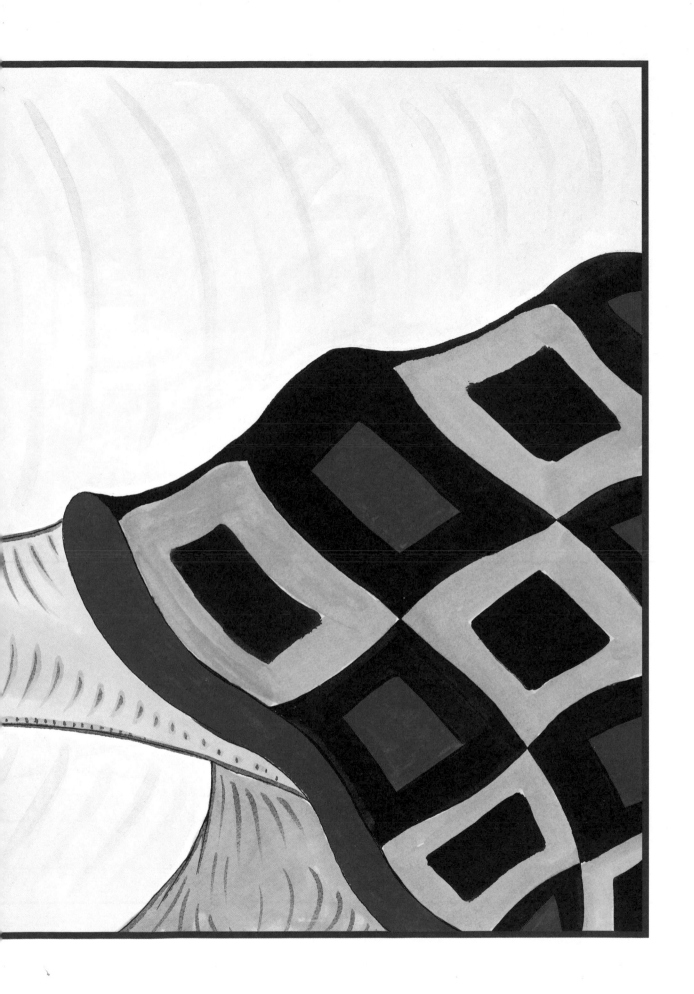

"But lately the humor has been drying up."

Bird took off. As he flew, he wondered,

"What did Turtle say?"

Bird saw Elephant. Bird said, "I just saw Turtle.

He told me the Watering Hole is drying up."

It takes a lot of water to quench an elephant's thirst.

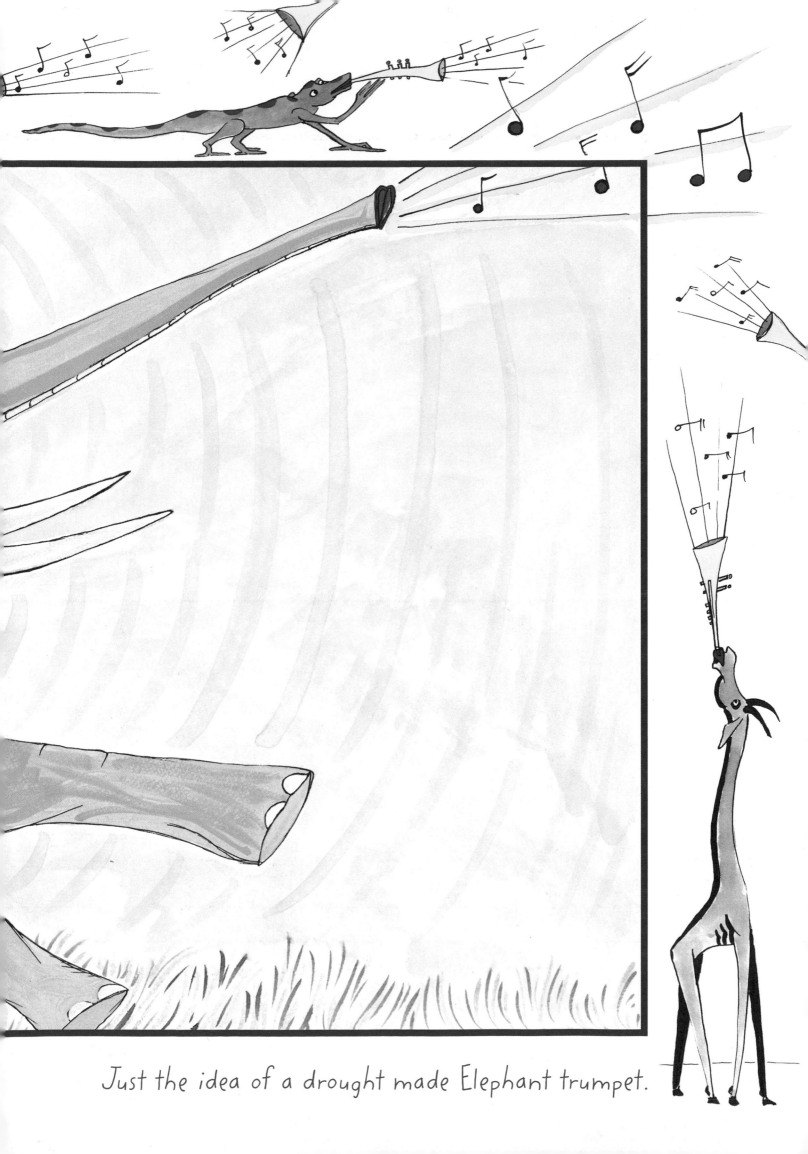

Just the idea of a drought made Elephant trumpet.

Elephant's trumpeting woke up Snake.
"What'ssss sssso excccciting?" he asked.

Elephant bellowed, "The Watering Hole is dry!"

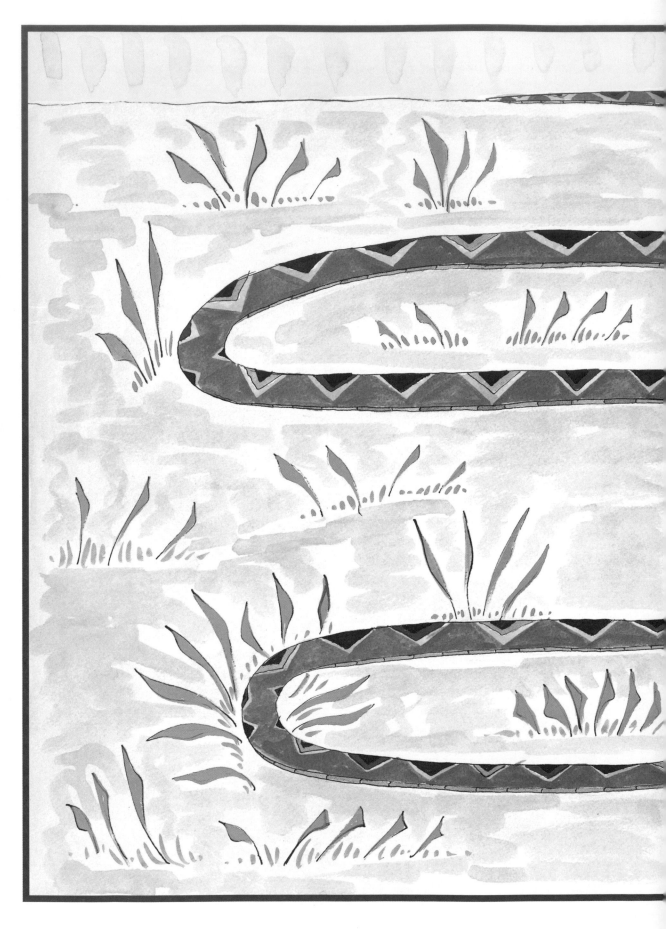

Snake slithered off to see for himself.

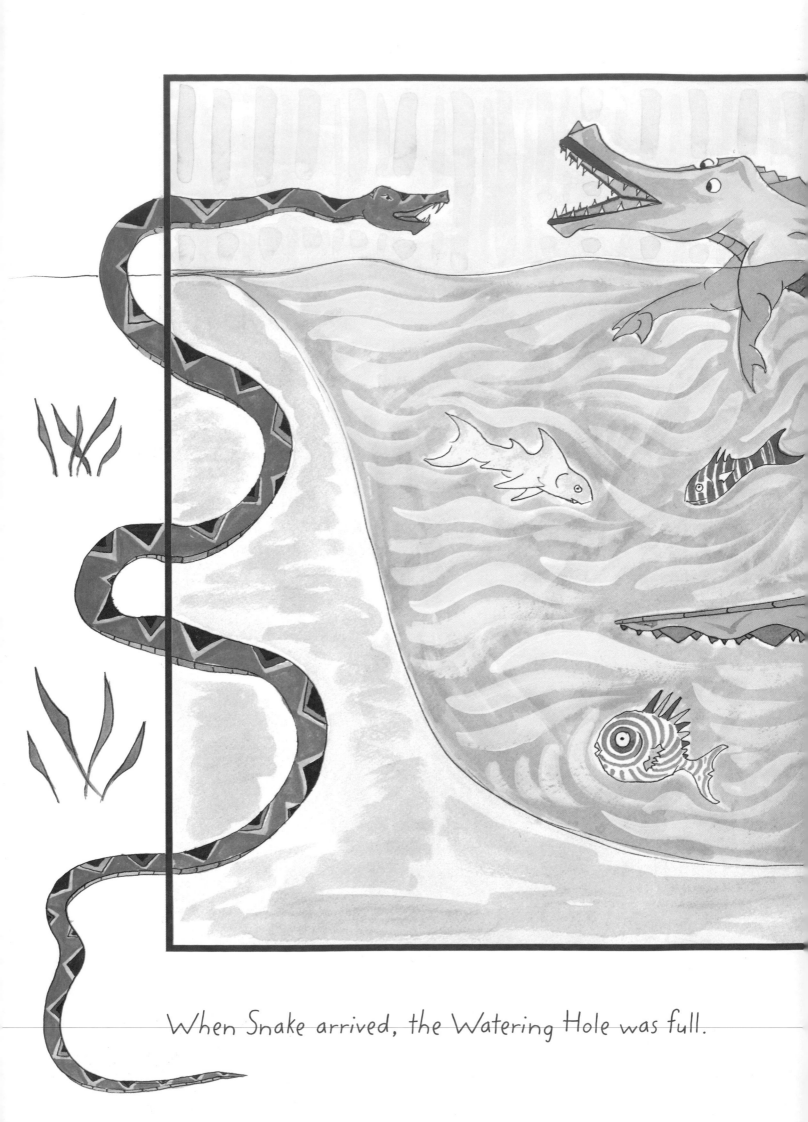

When Snake arrived, the Watering Hole was full.

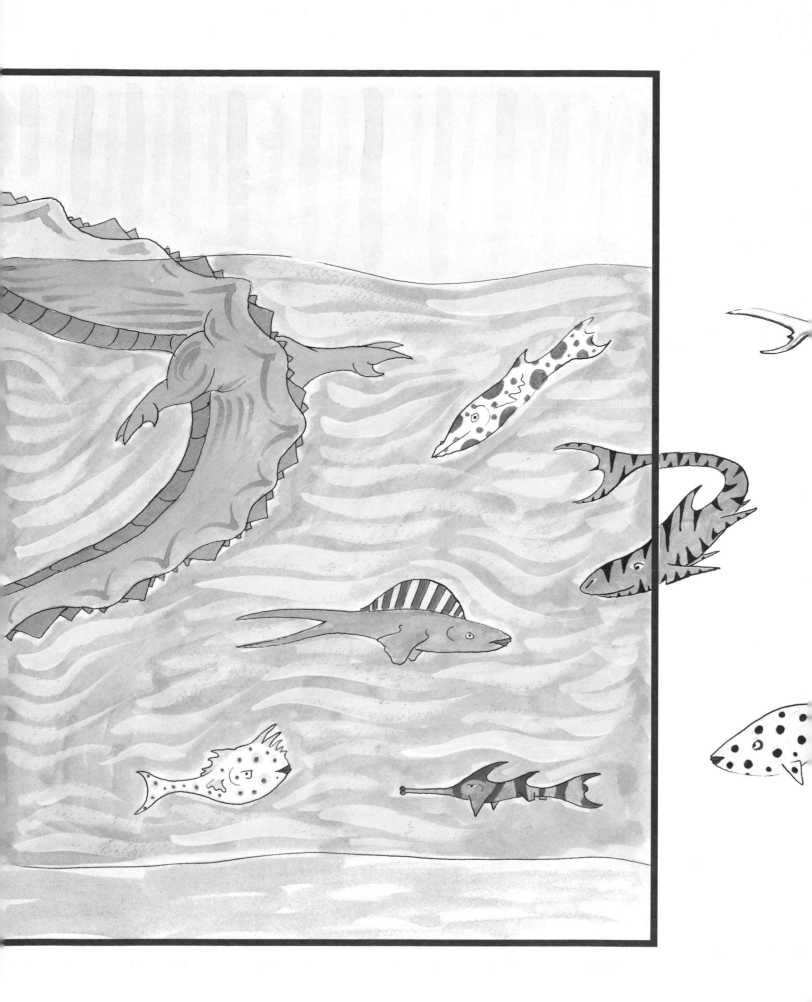

He told Crocodile, "The Watering Hole issss not too dry. It'ssss too high. If anything, it will flood."

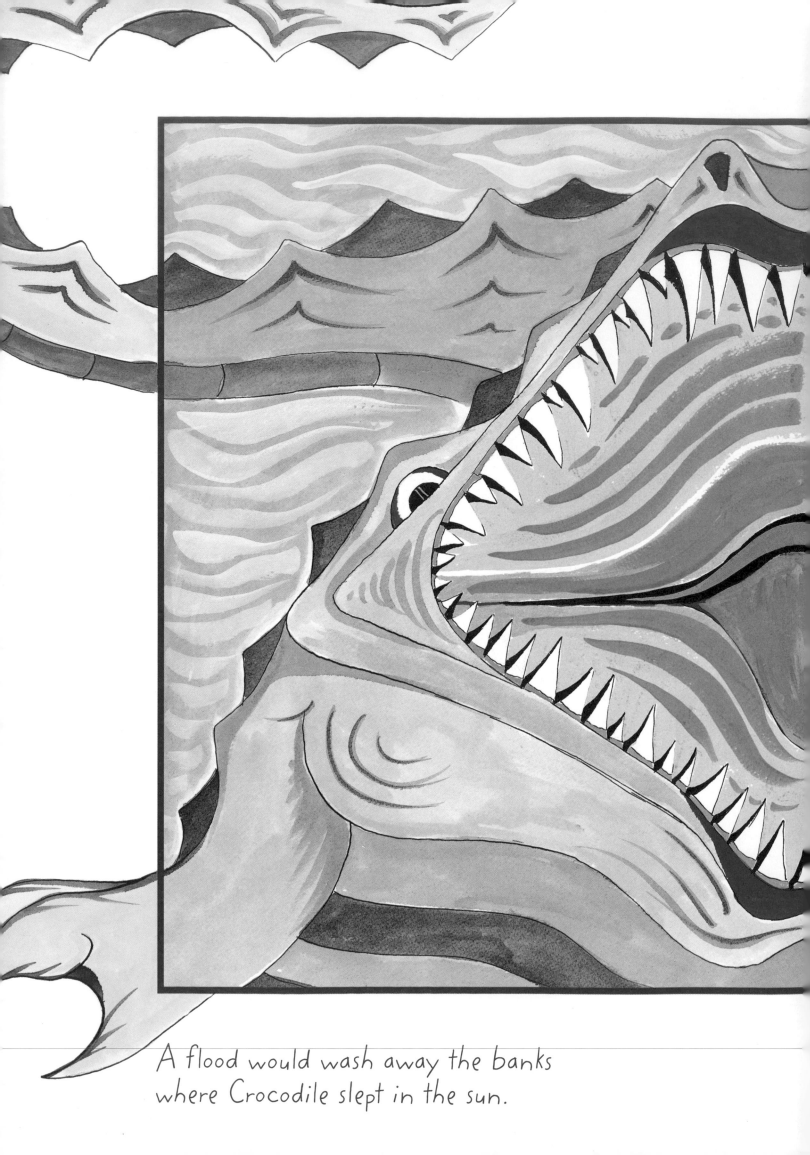

A flood would wash away the banks
where Crocodile slept in the sun.

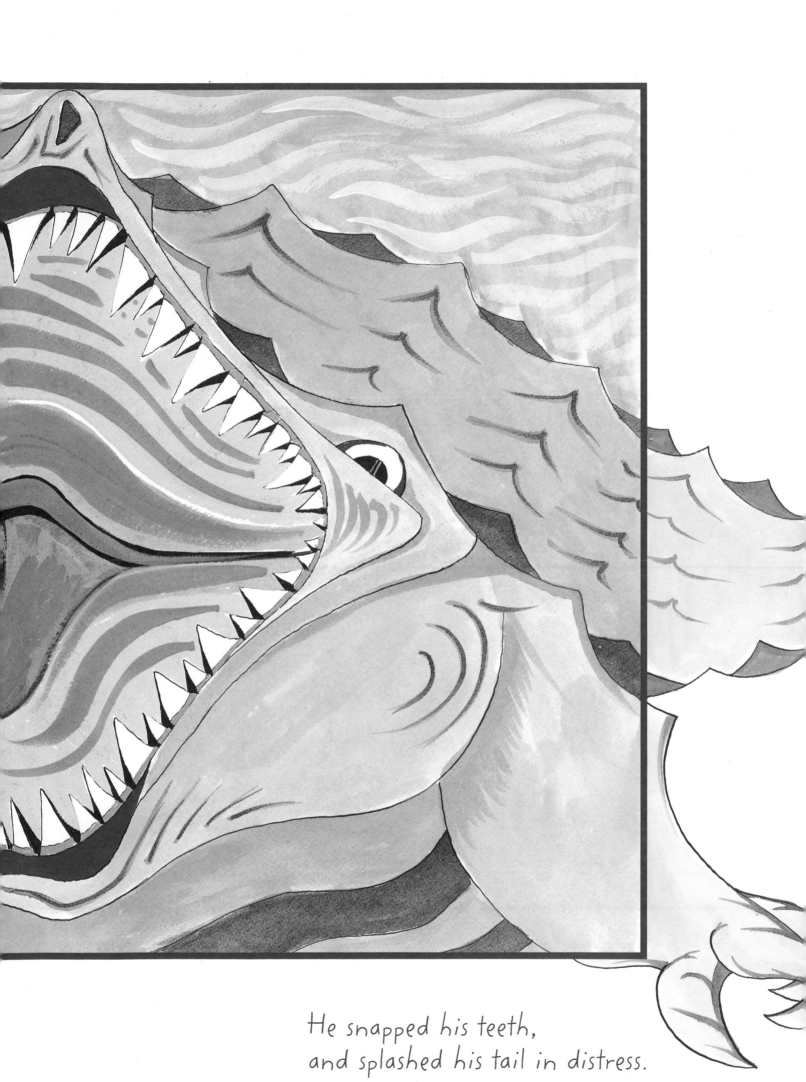

He snapped his teeth,
and splashed his tail in distress.

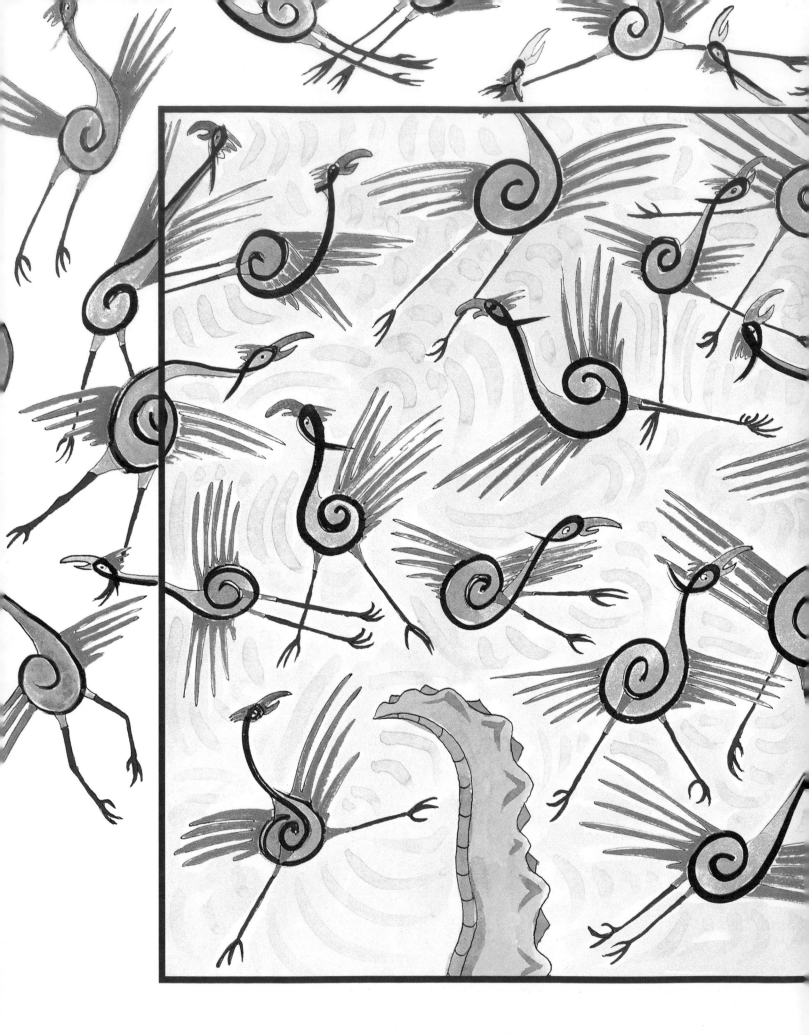

Crocodile's splashing spooked a flock of flamingos.

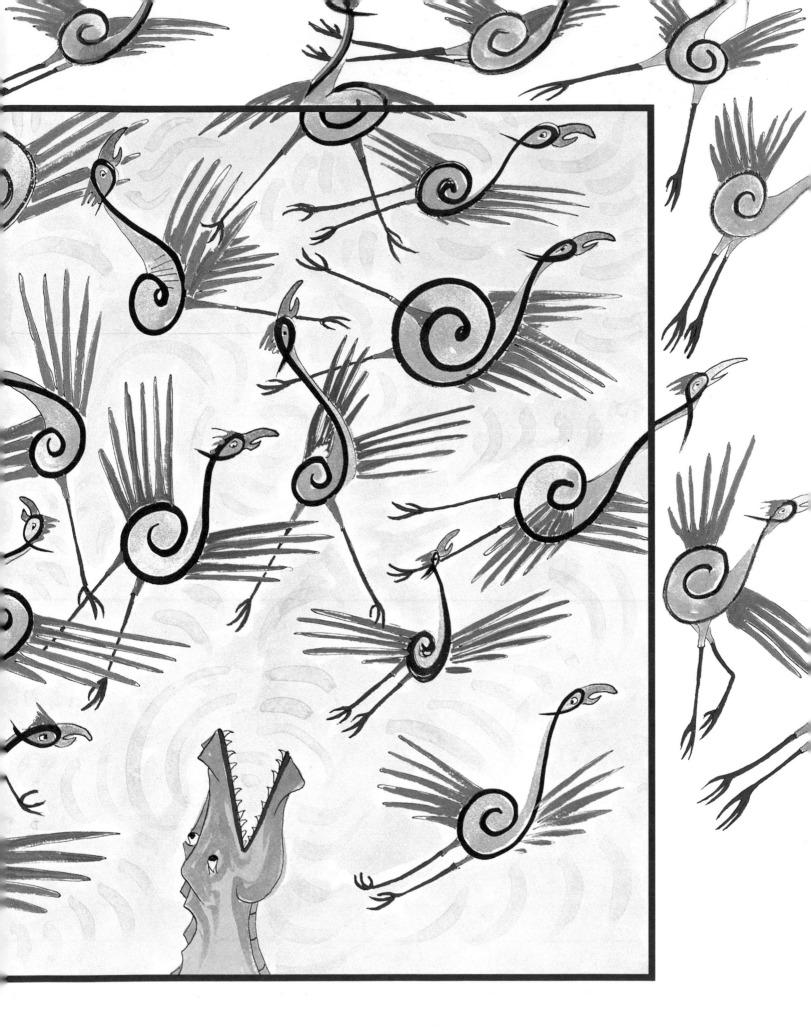

Taking flight, they filled the sky and called
a warning, "Croc! Croc! Flee! Flee!"

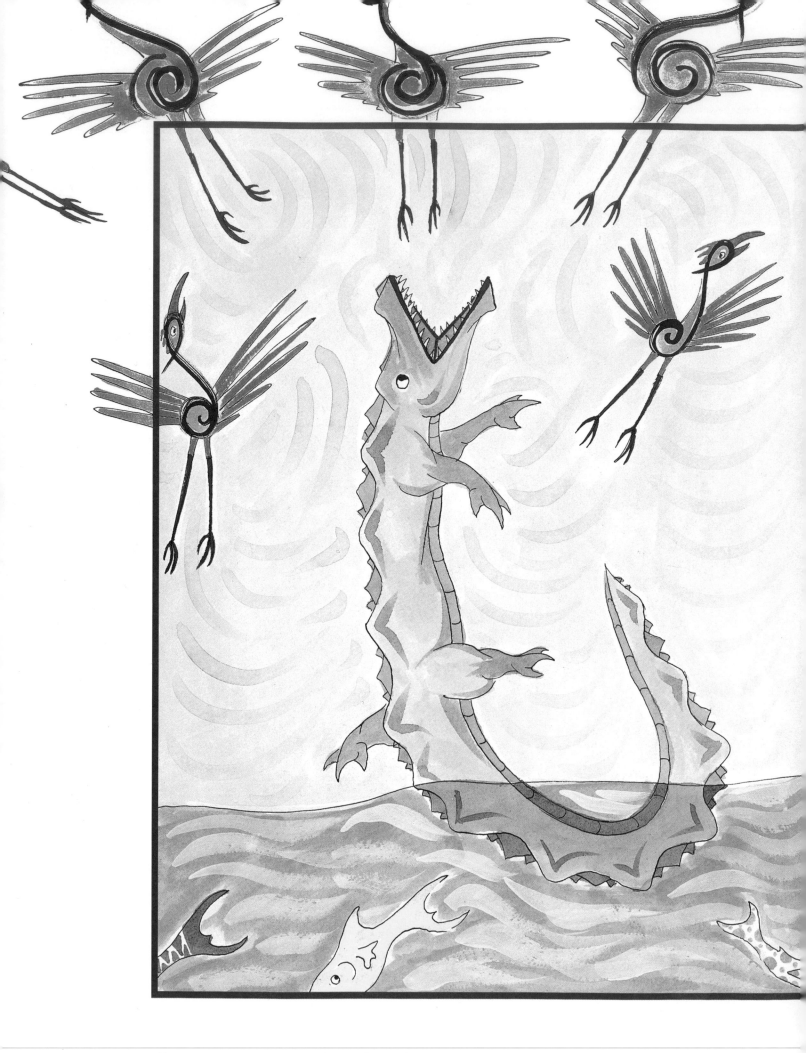

Crocodile thought the flamingos' warning was for him, proof that his fears of a flood had come true.

He shouted, "My gracious! It has begun."

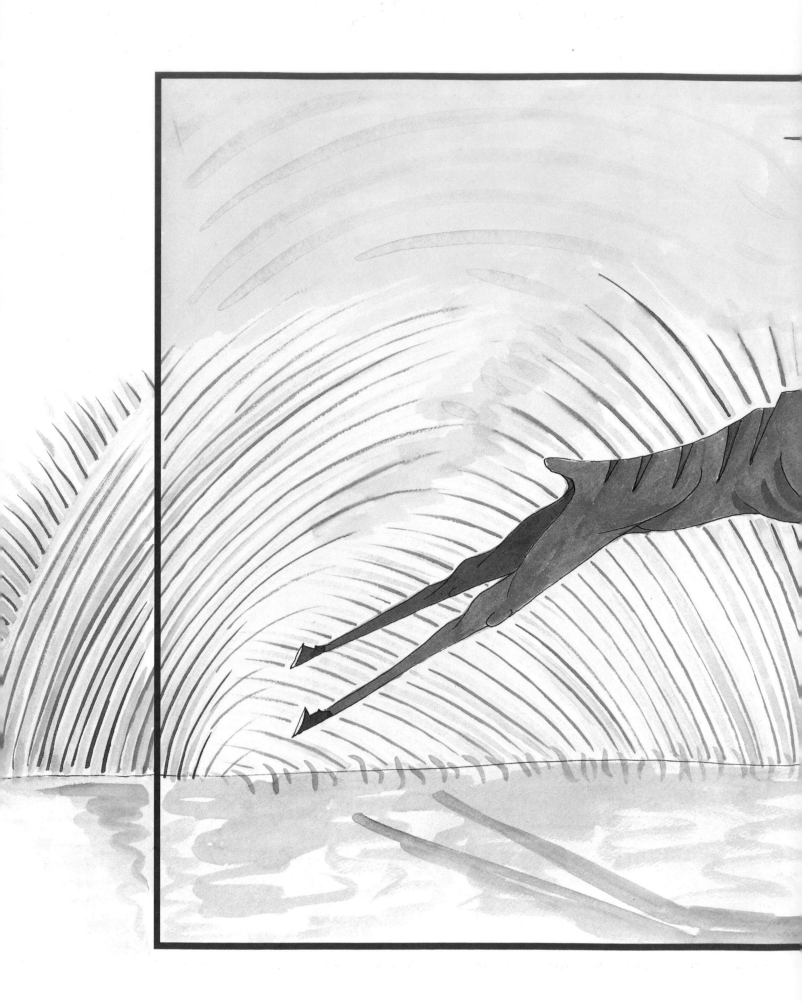

Gazelle was startled by the ruckus.

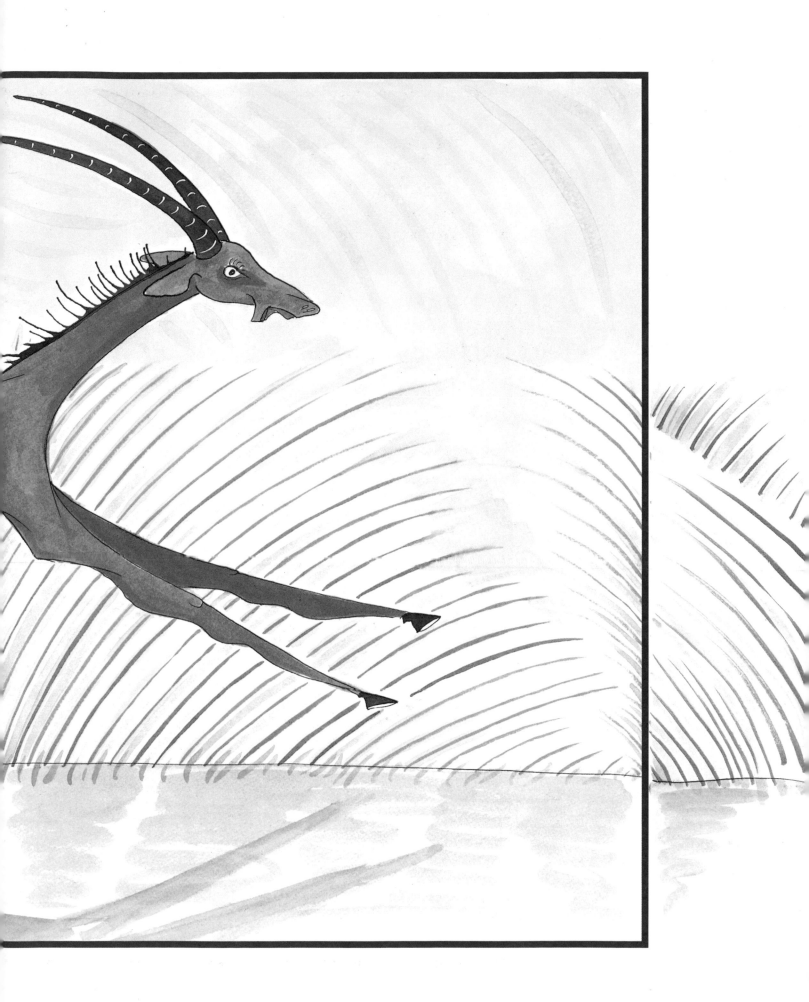

She sprinted off across the plains.

Gazelle saw Lion on the prowl. To save herself,
she repeated what she thought Crocodile had shouted.

Gazelle exclaimed, "The migrations have begun!"

For Lion, the migrations of zebra and wildebeest herds meant easy hunting.

He trotted off to the Watering Hole
to catch his dinner.

Of course, there were no zebras and no wildebeests at the Watering Hole. Instead, Lion saw Hippo.

Lion skulked back into the bush, grumbling,
"Don't believe everything you hear."

Just then, Bird swooped down.

He landed on Hippo's rump.

Hippo wallowed down. "I love the Watering Hole.

It puts me in such a good humor," he said.

Bird flew back to Turtle. "I was just at the Watering Hole," he said, "and Hippo has a good sense of humor."

Turtle laughed. "Hippo is funny. His jokes spread like wildfire, and when he gets going, there's no stopping him."

Bird took off again. As he flew, he wondered,
"What did Turtle say?

Something about a fire that can't be stopped!"

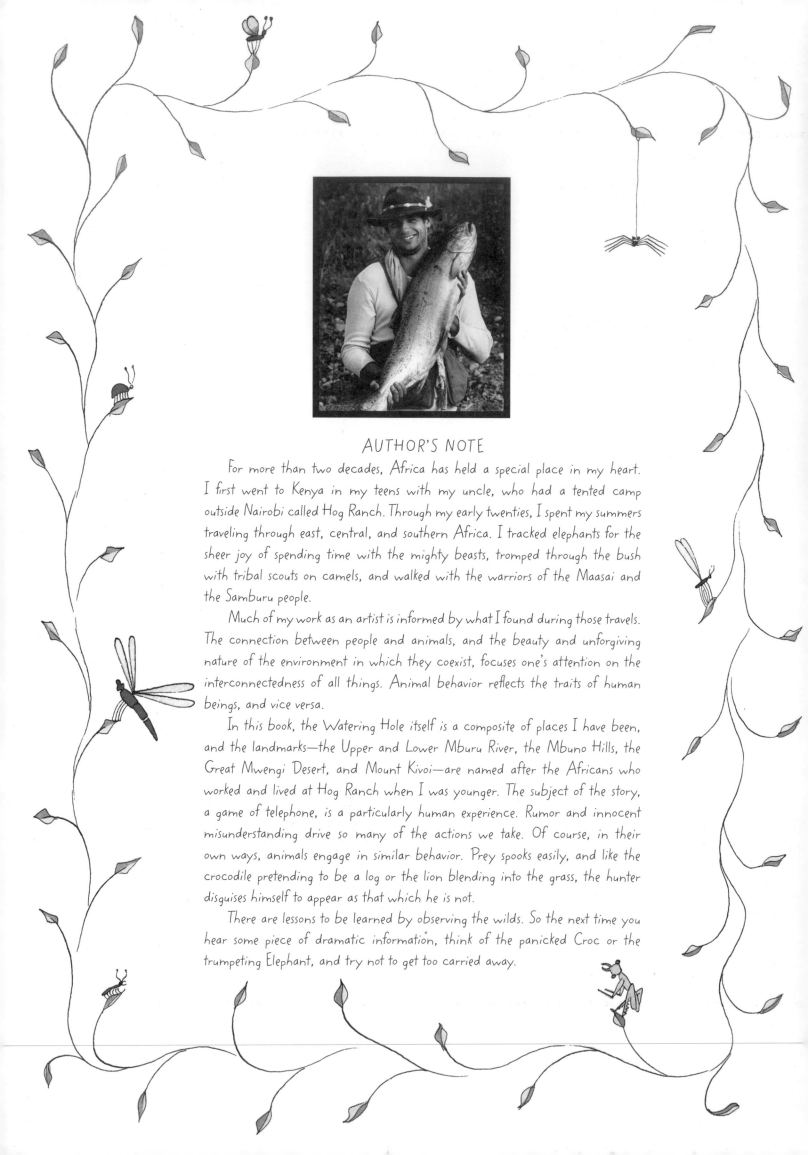

AUTHOR'S NOTE

For more than two decades, Africa has held a special place in my heart. I first went to Kenya in my teens with my uncle, who had a tented camp outside Nairobi called Hog Ranch. Through my early twenties, I spent my summers traveling through east, central, and southern Africa. I tracked elephants for the sheer joy of spending time with the mighty beasts, tromped through the bush with tribal scouts on camels, and walked with the warriors of the Maasai and the Samburu people.

Much of my work as an artist is informed by what I found during those travels. The connection between people and animals, and the beauty and unforgiving nature of the environment in which they coexist, focuses one's attention on the interconnectedness of all things. Animal behavior reflects the traits of human beings, and vice versa.

In this book, the Watering Hole itself is a composite of places I have been, and the landmarks—the Upper and Lower Mburu River, the Mbuno Hills, the Great Mwengi Desert, and Mount Kivoi—are named after the Africans who worked and lived at Hog Ranch when I was younger. The subject of the story, a game of telephone, is a particularly human experience. Rumor and innocent misunderstanding drive so many of the actions we take. Of course, in their own ways, animals engage in similar behavior. Prey spooks easily, and like the crocodile pretending to be a log or the lion blending into the grass, the hunter disguises himself to appear as that which he is not.

There are lessons to be learned by observing the wilds. So the next time you hear some piece of dramatic information, think of the panicked Croc or the trumpeting Elephant, and try not to get too carried away.

The illustrations in this book were made
with pen and ink and watercolor on paper.

Library of Congress Cataloging-in-Publication Data
Beard, Alex, 1970–
The jungle grapevine / by Alex Beard.
p. cm.
Summary: When Turtle makes an offhand remark to Bird at the Watering Hole one day, Bird's
misunderstanding starts a series of rumors that stirs up the other jungle animals.
ISBN 978-0-8109-8001-3
[1. Communication—Fiction. 2. Animals—Fiction. 3. Africa—Fiction.] I. Title.
PZ7.B3688Ju 2009
[E]—dc22
2008046197

Book design by Chad W. Beckerman

Printed and bound in China
10 9 8 7 6 5 4 3 2

Abrams Books for Young Readers are available at special discounts
when purchased in quantity for premiums and promotions
as well as fundraising or educational use. Special editions
can also be created to specification. For details, contact
specialmarkets@abramsbooks.com or the address below.

ABRAMS
THE ART OF BOOKS SINCE 1949
115 West 18th Street
New York, NY 10011
www.abramsbooks.com

The great Mwengi Desert

Bongo

Upper Mburu River

Turtle — Bird

Bird

Turtle to Bird

back to Turtle

The Leopard's Tree

Mt. Kivoi

Buffalo

Wildebeest & Zebra

grasslands

Lion to Hi...

N

W E

S

Lion

Giraffe

The Ant Hill